DODGING THE

SATANIC DARTS
OPERATING
THRU
IN-LAWS

I0678652

BY: SHANNON STAFFORD-AMOS

DODGING THE

SATANIC DARTS
OPERATING
THRU

IN-LAWS

BY: SHANNON STAFFORD-AMOS

Dodging the Satanic Darts Operating thru
In-Laws
Copyright ©2023 Shannon Stafford-Amos

Published by Never A-Mis Enterprises, LLC
P.O. Box 2298
Byron, GA 31008-2298
www.neveramisenterprises.com

ISBN: 9798985059786

*Printed in the United States
of America*

[7]

Reviewed by Dr. Carlos Juan Carmona-Goyena, PHD. By Kalpana M, MA, 2023, **Role of a Wife: 17 Things to do for a happy Marriage.**

Pastor Jimmy Evans, 2018, **Marriage on the Rocks,** *XO Publishing*

DEDICATION

I dedicate this book to my father in – love Melvin Amos, Sr., and my mother in– love Marlene Amos.

Melvin Amos, Sr, affectionally known as "Pops" … Thank you for loving me and accepting me AS IS! When I was thirteen years of age, you taught me a song and led me to believe in standing up and being a witness for JESUS! Since then, until now, I continue to do exactly that … be a witness for JESUS. Thank you. I love you. Continue in the blessings of the Lord.

Mrs. Marlene Amos, affectionally known as "Grandmom" ... Thank you for your tender embrace, your acceptance and love. Every gift you give me are dear and very precious to me. Your meek and quiet spirit speaks volumes. I decree continued blessings as you embrace all the Lord has for you. I love you.

PREFACE

Two of the services offered under "Families of Victory" umbrella is family support & Spiritual advisement sessions. As the director, I strongly believe in implementing the Word of God. The sessions are based off 1 Corinthians 15:57 **KJV**, *"Thanks be to God, which giveth us the victory through our Lord Jesus Christ."* We understand there will be trials and tribulations as long as we live. As a family unit, we have been graced to be victorious, as we fight from a seat of Victory! I give God all the glory for allowing me to sit and pen these thoughts, testimonies, biblical strategies, and prayers into the pages of this book. I am blessed to be able to share experiences I have encountered in over 30 years of ministry and over 25 years of serving the great state of Georgia residents in real estate.

I thought of the families and the crises leading them to my office for one reason or another. The marriages I have encountered have had issues due to outside folk trespassing in their marriage. Every couple has dealt with everyday life issues … BUT … there is vast majority of couples receiving direct satanic attacks flowing thru the hands of those whom they call "family"!

While preparing to pen my next book, we took a survey, and this subject was one of the top three on the list! In recent months it seems as if there has been an increase of inquiries, text messages, and prayer requests coming across my desk. Rapidly increasing couples are retiring; illness; and loss of employment. When the pandemic hit, it led people to dwell in their homes. Families started spending more time together daily. The couples were really getting to know their spouses; others encountered reality as to the type of person they married. There were other couples that weathered storms and embraced reality; the good and not so good. There were other couples that filed for divorce thus, they are no longer married. There are also couples who have reconciled and are taking the steps to heal their marriage.

We have been blessed to service families and individuals who have been displaced because of a traumatic event occurring within the family unit. Families of Victory has programs to service everyone in the family and address their needs through support groups; The Men of Honor; Women of Glory; and The Children of Promise.

Through the support group sessions and the transparency of all the attendees, hundreds of scenarios have come across our hearts and prayers.

Based off of a day-to-day contact with my office, the three key issues couples/individuals face are:

1. Understanding the Biblical order of the family unit chaos in the marriage.

2. The identity crisis of a Believer.

3. Singleness (where is my Boaz) I am tired of being single or going home alone.

We all know God is a God of divine order. The great deceiver comes to disrupt and distract the peace in our lives. When a family contacts our office with issues of this magnitude, the first thing we ask is how their walk is with the Lord. We realize not all families know Jesus as their Lord and Savior. Having asked such an important question, we seek how to best execute our mission. Our mission is to assist Families through the process of healing; from feeling like failures, to experiencing emotional, mental and Spiritual VICTORY!

Let us begin talking about chaos in the marriage… it comes with deep concern, sympathy, and love for the hearts of the people. Due to the deliberate and vicious attacks on their character, their hearts have been crushed, rejected, and broken. Sadly, these attacks came from those standing to witness their loved one unite in marriage and light the unity candle under God, to join two families; without *one* objection are

…THE IN-LAWS.

Love and marriage designed by God is a wonderful miracle. It is my prayer you are blessed beyond measure as you read this book. I pray your questions are answered as you embrace this book. I pray you will discover who the true enemy is, but in the end be encouraged and empowered to understand grace for change. I pray, as you embrace grace to experience change, you will go from just being an in-law to operating as one being bonded thru two people being in love...

Table of Contents

Table of Contents

Chapter One

Pre-marital Counseling.
Assessments.
Sessions.

Before the ring and the engagement

Marriage counseling sessions should be a pre-requisite to marriage for all. There are states and countries where pre-marital counseling is mandatory. Sessions are extremely important to the Believer that would like to be united in Holy matrimony. We have to take classes & tests before obtaining any type of license to operate, administer or function in a specific service. You have to have a license to work in a salon. Medical licenses are needed to be a doctor, nurse, or a patient care tech (Certified Nurse's Aids). Even as a medical billing and coding representative need classes and licensure. You cannot work on lights, plumbing, build houses to code or appraise houses without proper schooling and passing a state exam. Yet, people will jump into a lifelong commitment without asking certain questions, passing a communication exam, or meeting with Clergy.

There is wisdom in the multitude of counsel. During pre-marital counseling sessions, couples will gain answers to insightful information and answers to the what ifs, clarity of their prospective future mate's past, as well as goals for the future. It is during this time they will get to know their prospective mate on a higher and more intimate level. If the prospective mate is transparent and honest, their intimacy grow. Relationships founded on deception will come out of the gate with issues that will need to be ironed out before the marriage can really blossom into what God intended the marriage to be. It is difficult but doable. Most couples will even find out they can obtain a discount at the courthouse when applying for a marriage license if they have completed marriage counseling sessions. We strongly believe couples will have a better chance of their marriage surviving attacks that will come up against them, if they gain an understanding of the original intent of marriage. It is extremely important for the couple to be honest with one another prior to marriage. They need to be allowed to decide if they would like to continue with the relationship or not. It is robbery and unfair to them and their families to hide anything and be dishonest about anything they know will cause unnecessary heart ache, pain and/or grief. Life is already a challenge, adding additional stressors is inhumane, and can cause sickness, strife, and sometimes even death.

As Director of Families of Victory, pre-marital counseling is the greatest class we seek major interest in. We cannot stress enough the importance of pre-marital counseling sessions. Truth be told, you really do not know a person until you reside with them. Pre-marital counseling sessions help with the other factors. I am here to help! Families of Victory is here to help! Please understand, saying 'No' or not yet is better than a 'YES' and living a miserable life with someone you were not supposed to marry in the beginning; or someone who needed to finish developing in major areas of adulthood or womanhood prior to marriage. It is certainly better to receive a 'No' or not yet instead of being placed in a body bag or leaving lifelong emotional and mental scars in someone's life. Domestic violence is real and so is mental & emotional illness. It is dangerous to toy with the emotions of others. Serving in ministry and as an advocate, I have witnessed cases of nervous breakdowns, deaths, and violent acts due to the manipulation, deception, and unforgiveness in romantic relationships, which could have been avoided.

Pre-marital counseling is one of the services offered through Families of Victory Educational Center. Areas covered in detail during pre-marital counseling sessions at Families of Victory are:

- Religious Beliefs - Marriage, Church Attendance & Donations.

- Family Order - Husband, Wife, Children, In-laws.

- Ex-Spouses - Friends or Not, Communication inclusion- exclusion?

- The blended family orders.

- Children & Discipline - Hands on or off?

- Food & Hobbies - Eating out & friends?

- Employment - Outside of the home, Self-employment, second jobs etc.

- Finances - Money & Marriage, joint accounts?

- Counseling & Communication - Conflict Resolution- Arguments. The final Authority.

- Sex - How often? What style? Porn? Positions? What happens if we cannot?

- Medical & Death - Medical & Life Insurance Policies and expectations.

- Death - How would my spouse like to oversee their Home-going; Casket/Cremation?

- Housing – 5 - year, 10 - year, Retirement Home, Investments etc.

- Time Spent -Vacation - Time spent together or alone? With family & friends?

- Oneness -What is it? And the meaning of Amos 3:3, Exclusive/Non-Exclusive.

- Social Media - Phone's, emails, tablets, in boxing, and text messages?

- Standard Operating Procedures in the home. What is expected of each person in the home?

Engaging in premarital counseling will assist potential couples learn how to identify issues and handle conflict that will inevitably arise in their marriage. Premarital counseling sessions take anywhere from six weeks to ten weeks marriage. Take all the time you need prior to saying 'I Do.' In all your getting get an understanding.

Chapter Two

The order of the family unit.

We all know our Heavenly Father; Creator of the world, is the One Who founded the institution of marriage. He created humanity and established order when He did it. Man is first. The woman is second. The children the husband and wife created (even in a blended situation) are third. The Biblical order of the family unit is, God first, then the spouse, then the children. The spouses are one; because they are considered 'one flesh' – the responsibility to one's spouse comes first. The husband and wife take care of the kids even though their functions are different.

The purpose of marriage is to eliminate loneliness; to be fruitful and multiply; and have dominion in the earth. God created everything including man and said everything was "Good" He created. The only time God said something wasn't good is when He said, *"It's not good for man to be alone… (**Gen 2:18**)."* God caused a deep sleep to come upon Adam and took a rib and formed woMan. There were no spareribs, just *one* rib. When a man marries a woman, and takes her as his wife, he now becomes the head of the house. He is king of his own castle. *"For this cause a* *man shall leave his father and mother and cleave unto his wife ... (Gen 2:24). "* He is still his parent's son, his priorities as a man have to change. His number one priority is to God and then to his wife. The wife's number one priority is her husband, with God being ahead of him. Their marriage is now top priority, with God as the head of marriage. Nothing or no one should take precedence over one another. In the marriage vows, they both agree to, "forsake all others." This phrase is not just a statement, it is a vow they have made before God and witnesses! This vow is not only for people or the enemy of your marriage, but it also includes having to let go of their comforts.

A husband is to love his wife as Christ loved the church. Christ put His life on the line for the church! Jesus Christ was adamant about following His Father's instructions and completing His work here on earth. Husbands will not be able to complete their assignment as it pertains to the marriage. When he has the love of Christ in his heart, he will have an advantage those without Christ will not have. As the church submitted unto Christ, wives are to submit unto their husbands.

We must understand there is a difference between a man versus a man of God. There is absolutely no way to understand how to be a true husband or man without Christ. It is imperative husbands understand they are the faucet in which nourishment flows down to their wife/family. Man was birthed from God; woman was birthed out of man; children are birthed out of woman. If the flow of nourishment is followed, the family will be healthy and operate in its God given authority. As the husband submits to God, the wife will not have a problem submitting to him and the children see the original intent of the family unit flow. Now that the God-fearing atmosphere is created in the home, the family will operate in their God given assignments.

Sadly, there are times when a Jezebelic spirit is at work to cause confusion and fight against authority. This spirit doesn't want the family to operate in their God given assignments … We will deal with this in another part of the book!

Chapter Three

Too much negative chatter.

"Be not deceived: evil communications corrupt good manners (1Corinthians 15:33 *KJV*)." The information your in-laws, family, and friends receive regarding your household must come from those (little people eavesdropping and recording) within the household. The information repeated outside of the home came from inside the home!

Sometimes the spouse needs someone to vent to and they may open up to their parents or siblings, which may eventually lead to them talking about their spouse, which is never good. They are not contemplating leaving or filing for divorce, they simply want to vent. It is not as if they need help; they just want to vent. This puts the in-laws in an unbelievably bad position. This type of behavior will open doors for the spouse to be judged and ill feelings will begin to brew negatively against that spouse. This behavior also makes it hard for families to bond, especially if it is a blended family. You must remember the power in words and the enemy to the oneness of marriage would love to take those words and scatter them everywhere. Words are seeds which eventually yield fruit; in this instance, the words will yield negative fruit that will work *AGAINST* the marriage. The innocent venting is really the spouse's manners being corrupted, and those same words (seeds) are sowing discord. The spouse is causing heartache, harm, and pain to the listener, and the spouse being discussed.

The Bible says, *"Let no corrupt communication proceed out of your mouth, but that which is good to the use of edifying, that it may minister grace unto the hearers* **(Ephesians 4:29 KJV)."** Speaking evil or bad of your spouse does not edify them and does not administer grace to those listening.

It is causing strife; therefore, the spouse is not covering the heart of their spouse. Both of them are now a tool in the hands of the enemy of the marriage to cause harm and damage to the marriage; eventually their spouse could have a hard heart towards them. *Genesis 4:7 KJV* talks about how sin is crouching at the door. Sin is waiting at the door of your heart, waiting for you to unlock the door. Sin can crouch at the door as long as it wants, but for sin to come in, you must open the door, or have a little crack to get in!

Loose talking; false accusations; not telling the whole truth; or just releasing too much intimate information to others regarding your spouse can cause major problems, pain, and deep hurt to the marriage and your mate. There are occasions when the Holy Spirit filled in-laws will be led to pray, get specific insight from the Lord, and address certain issues. The Holy Spirit is a Gentleman, Who does not address issues to cause more confusion. The Holy Spirit will touch hearts to bring a resolve.

Discretion in marriage is one of the necessary tools to help build a successful marriage. It is not fair nor is it a good thing when your spouse does not have a strong mind or rooted isn't in Christ. The spouse that has been left uncovered or exposed to those outside of the circle of marriage will have to defend themselves against vicious attacks from the in-laws and all others with opinions. If you find yourself married to an articulate, alfa-female or alfa-male it is easy to be in the middle of war zone! It is the responsibility of the mates to cover for one another where the in-laws, and all others are concerned. No one should have permission to speak negatively or speak into your life regarding your marriage; your spouse, or your children without prior consent. If they speak negatively about your spouse, then they are speaking negatively about you and the God within you. *"Discretion will protect you; understanding will guard you…* **(Proverbs 2:11 NIV)."**

Chapter Four

Your enemies are never far away.

As I was studying and preparing to write this chapter, the following Scriptures were impressed upon my heart to share with you.

Ephesians 6:12 *KJV*

"For we wrestle not against flesh and blood, but against the rulers of the darkness of this world, against spiritual wickedness in high places."

Luke 12:53 *KJV*

"Father will be divided against son and son against father, mother against daughter and daughter against mother, mother in-law against her daughter in-law and daughter in-law against her mother in-law."

Micah 7:6 *NIV*

"For the son dishonors his father, a daughter rises up against her mother, a daughter-in-law against her mother-in-law – a man's enemies are the members of his own household."

Matthew 10:21-22 *KJV*

"And the brother shall deliver up the brother to death, and the father the child: and the children shall revolt against their parents and cause them to put to death."

Child of God there are snakes and

vipers among you. Snakes are **REAL!!** In

the Bible, snakes show up in Pharoah's court

(Exodus 7:12); in the wilderness *(Numbers*

21:7); on the island of *Malta (Acts 28:3);*

and of course, in the Garden of Eden

(Genesis 3:1). They are pictured as loathsome creatures, associated with poison and craftiness. Most people associate snakes with danger because they fear them. When people see snakes, they become paralyzed with fear. The average person does not know the difference between a poisonous or a non-poisonous snake, so fear is a natural reaction. Snakes are skilled at being sneaky and deceitful because they must catch their prey to survive. Snakes can transform themselves because they shed their skin frequently. Transforming is another way for them to disguise themselves.

I reviewed testimonies of marriages having severe problems with turmoil and deception was the underlying factor. The tension found between the spouse and their in-laws had one common spirit which was that of *DECEPTION*! The dreams shared with me often included snakes/serpents in their beds, surrounding their homes, or sleeping next to them.

I can remember one particular session when a wife who was also a woman of God, shared a disturbing dream with me … One morning she woke up praying in her Heavenly language. When she stopped praying, immediately she felt fear overtake her body. She noticed her husband's hands were clammy. His body was stretched out over hers and touching every part. She began to feel the bed moving back and forth in motion. When he opened his mouth, he began to hiss instead of speaking audibly. He finally got out the words, "Good morning" while choking and gagging at the same time. He reached for a bottle of water because he said his mouth was very dry. She told me she heard, "The spirit of the python is sizing you up for the kill and observing everything you do!"

She continued to cry and shake as she told me her dream. I got up and got a warm towel, wiped her tears, and then I embraced her. I reminded her of the authority she has as a Believer. As I was holding her, I spoke softly in her ear and let her know just as I was holding her, so was our Heavenly Father. I told her there was not anything that could pluck her out of His hands no matter how she is watched, sized up, or preyed upon! I began to decree, "No weapon formed against her would prosper!" I told her the truth was being revealed as to what she was dealing with in her dreams; there was no need to fear because as a Believer the Champion dwells on the inside of us. ***Luke 10:19 NLT*** says, *"Look, I have given you authority over all the power of the enemy, and you can walk among snakes and scorpions and crush them. Nothing will injure you."* As Believers, we must be mindful that our Father has given His angels charge over us to bear us up lest we dash our foot against a stone. Believers are not mere mortal men or women walking around defenseless and weak! God has given us the power to bind and loose. It is up to us to execute and take authority! We can put the enemy out wherever he is lurking. We must

take dominion and exercise our authority.

We must stop being bullied by the enemy …

Let God arise and every enemy be

scattered!!!

Chapter Five

How to protect your marriage
from meddling in-laws.

If someone is disappointed, it should be the in-laws, not your husband or wife. It is your job to manage your relationships with your parents, so they will not have the freedom to meddle in your marriage.

Sister-in-laws are like the other woman in the relationship. Although she may be your husband's sister, she is not his *WIFE*! It is the responsibility of your husband to set healthy boundaries. As a wife, remain in a secure place in God and in your marriage. It is your responsibility to walk in love and to remember she will always be his sister. Sometimes the husband becomes jealous of his brother-in-law. Don't forget they are men too. They have a deep connection with their wives and are often compared to each other. I often share in the FOV counseling sessions that we must seek peace with all men. *"If it is possible, as much depends on you, live peaceably with all men (**Romans 12:18 KJV**)."* Anything that disturbs your peace is too expensive.

Your spouse *MUST* take a stand – however they are still your family. You must encourage your spouse to maintain a healthy relationship with their family. God will work out the rest as you continue to pray and execute the plan of action when setting boundaries. Always be found in the right way of operating in the love of God.

Having a fourth person in the marriage is not necessary. *"And if one can overpower him who is alone, two can resist him. A cord of three stands is not quickly torn apart (Eccl. 4:12 NASB)."* God created male and female; and blessed them. Eve was created from Adam's rib. There were not any spareribs for backup or support! The spouses must decide they are the only team they will be … together. The ex will always be there, especially if there are children involved.

Parents will always be the parents, and siblings will always be the siblings … until the Lord calls us/them home. The family or an outsider only knows what your spouse has shared with them. It is imperative to put a guard around your mouth when sharing details about your marriage or your family's infrastructure. The family will still be judging your spouse even after you and the Lord have forgiven them! Family members must realize sometimes their loved one may simply want to vent or release steam. Marriage is between three; God, husband, and wife … *ONLY*! Saying "sorry" is not always good enough; there must be change. There is not anything too hard for God when there is a desire for change. *"How can two walk together unless they agree (Amos 3:3 KJV)?"*

Dear readers, remember the power you have once we have received Jesus as your Lord and Savior. You have the authority to bind and loose; you have your armor; Angels ready to be dispatched to war on your behalf; and most importantly you have an immensely powerful weapon called your tongue! It is time for us to use it for what we want to see by decreeing and declaring in

Jesus' name. God did it and so can we because He lives in us. Speak peace. Speak healing. Speak deliverance. Speak into your life. Speak into your marriage! Declare salvation. Decree wholeness. Break and bind division and loose unity. Here is the key, speak only what God has already said in His Word. Put Him remembrance of His Word. He promised to watch over His Word to bring His Word to pass. Angels are waiting to hearken only to the voice of God's Word. Remain encouraged as you guard your heart.

As you walk in love, you are asking God to help you through; His grace is sufficient. You are weak, but in God you are strong. He is the lifter of your head. You must run to the Rock that is higher than you. You need to ask Him to take your hand and breathe into your heart so you may be pure before Him. It is not easy, but it is necessary and worth it. Death and Life are in the power of the tongue, so you must be mindful of that which is spoken. You absolutely need the power of God to be able to make it through life and all the challenges it brings.

Chapter Six

"Satanic darts? This cannot be real … but it is!!!" … Let us drink "truth" serum.

(*True stories of firsthand experiences!).*

When you read the following true experiences, keep in mind it is not the person, but it is a spirit operating through the person. When two people divorce, the EX – is just that ... an ex-daughter-in-law or an ex-son in law. The two people are legally and spiritually separated, so they are no longer a unit. The relationship has been severed. Unfortunately, there are petty, evil, and messy carnal minded people walking around as "so called adults." Everyone hasn't grasped the concept of *"When I was a child I operated as a child. When I became an adult, I put away childish ways."* You also have to keep in mind satan is the real enemy, and he will use anybody who will yield themselves to him. He is a spirit, and he needs a body to function and operate on this earth. You will yield your body to God, or you will yield your body to satan. There is not a grey or middle area.

There are in-laws who are in their son's or daughter's marriage a little too much. During a divorce they can tend to take sides and have too much to say about the ex-spouse or the new spouse. There are cases the in-laws have tried to keep the ex-spouse around to keep the relationship intact or even provide a cloak (a covering to maintain the relationship between their daughter or son and their ex-spouse). Having minor children is a plus to this type of thinking, and true oneness is out the window. Remember, those who dislike boundaries are the ones who have none. God is a God of order. Marriage is honorable to God, and woe unto the person that puts their hand and mouth on the covenant in which God has brought together. My God, people must be careful. Let's get started with true stories of married couples who have experienced the situations previously

discussed.

It's time to take a sip of some "truth

serum" …

In-laws allowing the ex to spend the night.
Two newlyweds happily in love and married, they stop by their parent's house after returning from their honeymoon. When they get there, the stepmother in-law opens the door and greets him and his new wife. As the new wife walks through the door into the kitchen to have a seat at the table, standing in the kitchen is her new husband and the ex-wife bent overlooking in the refrigerator, in a sheer nightgown & robe. Yep, you guessed it, the ex-wife spent the entire weekend with her ex-in-laws. Imagine how she felt, and all the questions running through her head. To make matters worse, they called prior to stopping by the house. Their plane landed at eleven-thirty in the morning, and they did not arrive at the house until two in the afternoon. *LET US PRAY!*

Cloaking at its best!
Where is leadership and/or accountability?
In-laws covering to help the spouse operate in infidelity emotionally, spiritually, and physically?

The loving couple was scheduled to meet his parents for dinner that evening. He had business with his father, so he went in before coming back to bring the wife and kids. Once inside and ready to be seated, his parents, one of his uncles, and an unknown woman were already seated at the table.

Fresh flowers were next to the unknown woman, and the wife noticed and complimented her, asking, "What are we celebrating?" She hesitated; inhaled; exhaled, as if she did not want to answer ... then finally answered with a noticeable attitude and looking away at the same time "A friend gave them to me!" Immediately, the father started a conversation about the restaurant's rumored five-star service! The mother-in-law ignored her daughter-in-law and talked to the unknown woman the entire time, as if they were friends. Finally, the wife asks her husband, "How do you all know this woman?" The husband indirectly says she is a long-time friend of the family yet did not know her name; or he did not want to disclose it! He also continued to mention, "Mom's behavior was strange since she has been dealing with memory loss!" … Be careful what you speak into existence. *LET US PRAY!*

My place is available for you.

Phone rings … "Help me! My over caring in-law is always trying to get my spouse to visit alone." What is the purpose of getting your spouse alone? Is there someone else they want to introduce to them? They can't control my spouse anymore. I know they love and care for my spouse in their own way, but the enemy has them deceived into believing I am out to harm my own spouse! I wish they would allow us to love one another and stay in their own lane as a true Believer. There is always another person they are constantly introducing or reminding my spouse of; trying to encourage my spouse to leave our marriage. They curse our marriage by speaking negative words. They are constantly telling my spouse they can do better; telling my spouse their upstairs is always available for them whenever they are ready to move-in … When my spouse does not give into their tricks; they begin to verbally attack and hurl demeaning words while having a temper tantrum. It got so bad, my over caring and over-involved in-laws practically control the life of my spouse, that his EX is used as a pawn; the kids are used as a pawn; and money is offered; a pawn, and tool to control! At one point, they were at odds during their divorce, now they are the best of friends! The same caring in-laws were helping my spouse with his divorce back then with his EX, is now using the same EX to put a wedge between us! The oh so caring in-law is also using the EX to cause a riff and isolating my spouse from their entire family. I sense jealousy and envy! HELP! HELP! HELP!"

I had to remind her, "No weapon formed against your marriage shall prosper!" Walk in love and do not fear. Fear not the one that can harm the body, but the One that can harm the body and the soul. I reminded them of Jermiah 15:11, "Surely I will deliver you for a good purpose; surely I will make your enemies plead with you in times of disaster and in times of distress." *LET US PRAY!*

Will the real spouse please stand?

"No matter what holiday it is, my wife's ex-husband is going to attend the family event at my in-law's home. He even parks his car when he goes out of town. He is called on to do favors family members. He knows the family business as it unfolds. He is at every birthday, anniversary, and in-law celebration. Is it me, or am I just a jealous husband? Do they like him better than they like me? Wait… Why am I even thinking this way? Is there unfinished business between the two of them? I am not a man who cares. Or should I care? My pride and ego are on the line, so do I discuss it? Or is this the norm? Am I wrong?

My wife and I agreed to be transparent, so I need to be open and honest about my feelings. She is a woman of prayer. I have witnessed the Holy Spirit reveal so much to her, while we are praying. God shows her something in her dreams and it happens. One of our kids may not be telling the entire truth, and the Holy Spirit will reveal to her exactly what happens or what happened. What is really going on here? I know she loves me, but why is this man always around?

If he wants the children, he should have someone drop them off and pick them up; he has every other weekend visitation! Why can't he visit my in-laws on days I am not there? I need help … I'm being a petty "Peter Pan"! I was told to look past it, but I simply cannot. Doesn't he have a new life? Can't he find new in-laws? I am asking for a friend, named ME! It got so bad that her relatives from out of town were saying, "I heard you got remarried, but where is he?!" They did not know who I was; and it seems like she does not want them to know either. I felt like she could change that if she wanted to. When I asked her about it, she responded, "That is just how they are. You know my folks."

I feel hurt; alone; lied to; cheated on; misled; deceived; confused; out of the loop; and the bunt of a huge joke everyone knows about except me! I have talked to a counselor, and they have agreed with me. It is also not good for the children to give them false hope, thinking their parents are going to reconnect or rekindle the relationship. I love my wife and I know she loves me, but this situation keeps me on my knees praying for clarity. Do I want him to find a wife and a new family? Or ... is my wife operating with the mindset of being in an open relationship? Is she trying to introduce "swinging" into our marriage, a marriage with no boundaries? ... I am totally confused. Why can't my in-laws who are Christians see what they are allowing to be done to me? To our marriage? Do they even care? Help me please! I can't do this alone! I am tired of hurting." *LET US PRAY!*

Suffer not the witch to live~The spirit of Jezebel must DIE!

The phone rings and the conversation go like this, "Woman of God, I promise you I cannot make this stuff up … Only the strong shall survive, so I just keep on living. The in-laws really want to break up the marriage. A month after the wedding, they offered to pay for an annulment! How cruel can someone be! Someone had one too much to drink, so I totally ignored the gesture. Sadly, it was just the beginning of a string of attacks against our marriage. One of the in-laws and my spouse sale cars at different dealerships, and the other in-law gifts the stepchildren large sums of money to make major purchase at the other in-law's dealership. They also go out of their way to make sure my spouse does not find out about what they did! It is not just one transaction. It is multiple transactions right up under our nose. How! you think that made my spouse feel when they found out their family was operating in such a manner? Creating a wedge yet hiding their hand while doing it!" Side note … Be incredibly careful about serving mammon!
LET US PRAY!

It is a grand celebration, and my spouse is not invited.

Phone rings again ... "Woman of God, I told you I cannot make this stuff up! My in-laws retired and decided to throw a surprise celebration that would be a birthday, an anniversary, and reaching a milestone. This was going to be a celebration to remember. At one point both spouses were welcomed in the where the celebration was taking place. A previous invitation to another celebration was extended, but none was extended for this one?! Everyone in the family, friends, ex-spouse's; and even people we did not know; even the EX-spouse was invited ... but not the current spouse.

It went a little like this: Overly involved in-law orchestrates everything; location of celebration. My ex-spouse; on the mic and over the music, sitting front and center. The ex-sister on deck; covering the catering and décor for the event. Family from everywhere are coming to celebrate. The other overly involved in-law did not utter a word to either of us regarding our parents' celebration! How _REDICULAS_ is that?! To make matters worse, one of our distant relatives called and requested our presence at the event we knew nothing about. It does not matter, because my unwanted spouse is asked to leave by the over involved in-law … after EVERYBODY else is welcomed!

Finally, the host agrees with the demands of the over involved in-law and asked the unwanted spouse to leave the premises.

After they asked my unwanted spouse and I to leave, they reassured us that the gifts being sent to the grandchildren are welcomed and appreciated.

We could hear the blessing over the food being said as we were leaving out the door, which made it even more bittersweet. We caught a glimpse of one of the relatives whose eyes were swelling up with tears and shaking her head out of disbelief.

My uninvited spouse turned and headed to toward car; although I wanted to remain … there was no way I ought to I deeply loved my spouse! I was wounded by the behavior of the over involved in-law and embarrassed by the family behavior.

Of course, my ex-spouse reached.

out (in violation of the of the agreement the three of us produced) begging me to return to the celebration. He said it looked bad for him to be on the MIC and the child of the honoree is gone. I am thinking to myself, "What was the purpose of the ex-spouse being there instead of my current spouse?" I forgot to mention the salesperson, the childhood friend to the over involved in-law was there front and center! Yet my spouse was …

Never mind! The over-involved in-law had the audacity to call and express their disappointment about not having any pictures of me with the rest of the family. The sad thing is the over involved in-law had them follow their "religion." Did the over involved in-law forget the couple was never invited to the event? Or were they trying to save face by mentioning they did not get any pictures, because was never going to be pictures?!"

Tricks are for kids' silly rabbits! Mother has always encouraged her children to never go where they are not invited. Always take the high road. God will contend with those who contend with you so says the Lord in Isaiah 49:25. *LET US PRAY!*

Not safe in our home – Eyes among us.

I get another phone call … "Woman of God, you will not believe what is going on now … I found recordings which looked as though they came from a type of nanny cam. These days, teenagers are always leaving stuff behind. I took it to a friend of mine who works at a lab, and they said it was a recording device! First there was a tracking device found in my car, now this little thing!

Once the nanny cam was examined you will not believe what was on it! … For starters, an entire conversation and photos of my new spouse and the children as they were headed

on vacation to Mississippi. There was a conversation about how the children felt about their parents divorcing. Questions were asked of the children, what would they do if the spouse got divorced again and they got a new stepparent. WHY? There were even recordings of certain conversations.
being held at the dinner table. Pictures. More conversations. What could be going on in their minds? No conversation is safe in what is supposed to be the comfort of my own home … Right …NOT! Sadly, one is not comfortable in their own home."
All things work together for your good according to Romans 8:28. *LET US PRAY!*

Chapter Seven

Let us pray.

Let Us Pray...

Forgiveness Prayer

Lord, I come to You now in the name of Jesus. Heavenly Father, today I choose to walk in forgiveness. I forgive _____ for anything they may have done or said to me or about me. I release them to you, and I ask you to bless them right now in Jesus' name. Heavenly Father, I ask You to forgive me for any hard feelings I have had towards them and to fill me with Your love for _____ in Jesus' name. I cannot do this in my own strength, so I am leaning on You Holy Spirit to help me. Heavenly Father, I am also asking You to forgive _____ for any unforgiveness they have in their heart towards me or others. I ask You to bless them in Jesus' name. I believe and receive answers to this prayer. I rest in the finished works of Jesus Christ to bring it to pass. To God be the Glory!

Forgiveness of Others

Lord God, I forgive anyone who has ever wronged me; hurt me; spoke evil of me; lied to me or on me; tried to harm me in any way. I pray You bless them. I ask You to forgive me for any unforgiveness; bitterness; anger; strife; animosity; or resentment I may have in my heart toward anyone at the time. In Jesus' name I pray ~ Amen.

Unity Prayer

Eternal God our Father, I come to You now thanking You for instilling in me Your abiding love for all people regardless of who they are, or differences they may possess. They are all a part of Your creation. I pray You give us wisdom to relate to them, according to Your will, plan, and purpose for their lives. Allow us to help keep Jesus on display and show forth the true face of Christianity while encountering people. Let us know Your purpose for them placed in our path, and what ministry each one needs. Lord, help me show all people unconditional love. You show regardless of how they treat me. I yield to Thy will being done in my life. In Jesus name, I declare unity, peace, love, and joy shall abide in my home and in my relationships. I choose to believe and receive answers to this prayer in Jesus' name – Amen.

Loose and Let go of Resentment and Bitterness Prayer

My Lord my God, I need Your help. I come to You by the shed Blood of Jesus Christ. Father, help me let go of all bitterness, anger, strife, and resentment. You are the One Who binds up and heals the broken hearted. I bring my heart to You to heal and bring back all the fragmented pieces of my soul back together. I receive Your anointing which breaks and destroys every yoke of bondage. By faith, I receive Your healing according to Your Word. Lord, I realize I have a right to be healed because of the stripes Jesus took on His back for me. Thank You for sending me Your Holy Spirit to comfort me during this moment in time. I acknowledge the Holy Spirit as my Wonderful Counselor. Holy Spirit, guide and lead me as I maneuver through this season of my life. I choose to forgive those who have wronged me. I choose to live a life of forgiveness because You have forgiven me. I repent of all bitterness, anger, strife, and resentment; along with any form of malice or slander that may have been attributed to me. I choose to release all negative feelings in Jesus' name. Holy Spirit, I need Your help as I make every effort to live in peace with everyone. I am seeking You. I am looking unto You, the Author and Finisher of my faith. Help me watch and pray so I will not enter temptation or cause others to stumble. Thank You Heavenly Father for watching over Your Word to perform it. I declare I have overcome bitterness and resentment by the Blood of the Lord Jesus Christ. Thank You, Lord for restoring unto me right now the joy of my salvation. Glory to God on high! I refuse to be angry and waddle in self-pity. I accept my assignment and continue to press forward in the name of Jesus. I refuse to take my eyes off Jesus. Hallelujah! I am loved. I am accepted. I am more than a conqueror. No more bitterness … no more resentment … only LOVE! Thank You for manifesting love in my life right now in Jesus' name – Amen.

Binding and Loosing Prayer

Almighty God in Heaven, I come to You as humble as I know how, yet boldly to obtain mercy in my time of need. I thank You for the armor You have given me to fight against the wiles of the enemy. I know the weapons of my warfare are not carnal but mighty in pulling down strongholds. I thank You for honoring Your Word. You told me whatsoever I shall bind on earth shall be bound in Heaven; and whatsoever I loose on earth shall be loosed in Heaven. In the name of Jesus and with the authority You have given me, I bind satan's evil efforts, evil principalities, powers, rulers of darkness, and wickedness in high places. Father, Your Word says You are my Deliverer. I ask for manifestation and total deliverance from anything that is not like You Lord. Thank You for manifesting diving healing and divine health. Thank You for manifestation of every miracle and every healing You have for me. It is You Who knows the plans You have for me, and I submit my will so Thy will may be done in my life. I thank You for directing my path and making every crooked place straight, bringing down every high mountain. I loose joy, contentment, peace, and love to operate fully in my life right now in the name of Jesus. May all things done be used to glorify You Lord. Thank You for not only hearing but answering my prayers and showing me great and mighty things, I know not of. I believe and receive what I have prayed for – Amen.

Prayer to stop Deception.

Lord, I come to You through the Blood of my Lord and Savior Jesus Christ. Thank You for revealing deception in full operation. Lord, thank You for destroying and removing any deception in my mind. I ask You Lord to reveal all trickery and deceit. Let all hidden things be revealed. Lord let all forms of deceit be exposed. Allow me to see through the haze, smoke screens, schemes, and the plans of man and the enemy; to know only Your truth. Thank You for allowing Your angels to guard me and keep me safe from those coming against me. I take authority over all sickness, disease, and physical maladies. I speak divine health over, in and through me. I declare total chemical and mental balance over, in and through my body. I decided to maintain what You have already obtained for me. With Your strength and help, I choose to put on a sound and sober mind, long life; longevity in the spirit and mind all the days of my life. I loose my angels to eradicate, annihilate and obliterate every diabolical plan and scheme of the enemy and all dark forces. Lord, I ask You to strengthen me and protect me all areas of my life. I ask You for Your Spirit to abound in and through me abundantly. Lord, keep those from who You do not want me. I pray my sleep will be sweet and restorative. Cause me to rest and not be stressed. Fill me with rivers of freshness every moment of every day. You and You alone will order my steps for Your name's sake. Let peace infill me. Bring me into Your secret place, Your loving presence. With Your tender mercy, comfort my soul. In Jesus' name I pray – Amen.

Prayer for Husband & Wife to Strengthen their Struggling Marriage.

All Wise and All-Knowing God our Father. We come bowed down to worship, honor, in adoration of You. You alone are God, Creator of heaven and earth. You alone know who we are the purpose in which You created us. We pray together seeking Your wisdom as husband and wife. Thank You for Your Holy Spirit comforting us during this season of our marriage and showing us Your plan of action for us. Not our will, but Your will be made manifest now. The Holy Spirit help us to rediscover the joy, peace, love, and unity we once experienced in our union. Release Your angels to close unknown doors that we may have opened to cause division and separation. Remove people from our path that are enemies to the oneness of our marriage. Cause our ex-spouses to move on with their lives in other healthy relationships and friendships. Correct our in-laws and place them in their rightful position in our lives. Quicken our hearts when we see things out of order. God, forgive us for allowing anything and anybody to come between our marriage. Forgive us for having any other god in our lives other than You. Thank You Lord for teaching us Your divine order for marriage. We lean on You to speak to us. Help us to always put You first, and then our marriage over everything. Lord help us re-examine our commitment in the light of Your love for us. Thank You for another opportunity to get it right. We declare and decree wholeness, oneness, and unity with us. We declare and decree our marriage be restored right now in Jesus' name we pray – Amen.

Prayer for Restoration of Marriage.

Father, I thank You that You hear my prayer. I hold fast to Your promise to hear and answer my prayers. Thank You for inclining Your ear to hear the cry of Your beloved. I come in the name of Jesus and the authority of Your Word. I come boldly to the throne of grace to receive mercy and find grace for Your help in restoring my marriage. I take my place, standing in the gap for my husband (wife) against the devil and his demons. Father, I have forgiven him (her) of his (her) shortcomings and transgressions just as You have forgiven me. I stand firm knowing the Holy Spirit will convince and convince him (her) of their wrong. Help me Lord to remain sane and sober-minded, temperate, and disciplined because I love my husband (wife) and I remain committed to the covenant of our marriage. Lord God, I pray _____ will be delivered from this present evil age by the Son of the Living God. Whom the Son makes free is free indeed. I ask for manifestation and deliverance from the spirit of rejection and to have assurance of being accepted in the Beloved being holy and blameless. Lord, I come humbly before You, asking You to heal this broken marriage as Jesus came to heal the broken-hearted. You promised us in Your Word if we believe in the Lord Jesus Christ, we would be saved, and our household would be saved. Help us to submit one to another as submit ourselves to You. Heavenly Father, I ask You to rebuke any plans of the enemy to keep this family apart. We know Satan and his assigned imps come to steal, kill, and destroy. We stand firm and confident knowing he has no power over You, Lord. We cling to the abundant life in full operation, specifically in our marriage. Thank You Father for hearing my prayer on behalf of my marriage and family unit as we strive for Your love to reign supreme in our house; for Your peace to function as umpire in all situations. We declare and decree You to be Lord over our household. You are Lord over our spirit, soul, and body. Thank You for restoration and being our God. Thank You for not leaving or forsaking us. Thank You for loving us and guiding us along this journey. We glorify You. We magnify Your Hoy and Majestic name. To You be all the praise and honor due unto Your Holy name. We release our most

holy faith to bring this prayer to pass. As we rest
in His finished work. In Jesus' name – Amen.

Prayer to Bless the Marriage.

We thank You Lord, for the love You have
imparted in my heart and _____'s heart. Lord,
help me to always show love, honor, and respect.
Lord, show me how to be considerate of
_____'s feeling and always be concerned for
_____'s needs and desires. I need You Holy
Spirit to guide me and help me to understanding
and forgiving of _____'s weakness and
shortcomings. Thank You Lord for blessing our
marriage with peace and happiness. Make our
love fruitful so we will be an example of Your
Glory to everyone we encounter. Lord, thank You
for _____ being the love of my life and
walking in oneness with me! In Jesus' name –
Amen.

Chapter Eight

The conclusion of the matter.

Marriage is an honorable estate and instituted by God signifying unto the mystical union between Christ and His Church. As the gates of hell shall not prevail against the church, woe unto to the one that comes against or between the marriage covenant. Contending with marriages is to contend with God because He is the middle cord of a three-fold strand. Let no one attempt to separate or divide those whom God has joined together. As a Believer, we must remember to walk in love, with discernment and integrity. Earnestly pray for one's enemies. Love is patient, love is kind;

it does not envy; it does not boast; it is not proud; it is not rude; it is not self-seeking; it is not easily angered; it keeps no record of wrongs. Love does not delight in evil but rejoices with the truth. It always protects, always trust, always hopes, always preserves. Love never dies. Love covers a multitude of shortcomings. I have listed a couple of songs the Holy Spirit placed in my spirit:

Ce Ce Winans – *Believe for it.*

Tamela Mann – *Take me to the King.*

Tamela Mann – *Help me.*

Whitney Houston – *I look to You.*

Elevation Worship – *Jireh.*

***Elevation Worship** – I shall want not.*

Allow me to declare and decree; bind and loose somethings, in and over your life. Whatever you are doing in life, carve out at least an hour a day for thirty (30) days to worship and pray over your marriage and for your in-laws.

Repeat after me:

We bind division, strife, and envy. We loose love, peace, and joy in Jesus' name. We bind the spirit of Jezebel and cancel the plans of the enemy. We loose the hounds of Heaven to attack and the spirit of Jehu in Jesus name! We bind ever negative word spoken over our marriage. We loose the Angels of God to battle in our behalf as they encamp about our dwelling. We declare and decree our marriage wins in Jesus' name. We declare and decree salvation, healing, and deliverance in our family in Jesus' name. We decree and declare nobody, but Jesus sits on the throne of our lives. In Jesus name.

Nuggets:

- *Remain positive. Saying "Yes" to happiness leaves no room for the silent killer called "stress."*
- *Choose to live your life pleasing unto God and be free from the bondage of people.*
- *Refuse to break. Take care of your mental, physical, and spiritual health.*
- *People need accountability and prayer partners.*

Quotes:

"True oneness in marriage cannot be experienced if you allow in-laws to penetrate the circle. If necessary, let them become out-laws. It is crucial that you establish boundaries."- **DeBorrah K. Ogans**

"Then she told me, "You have changed my son." Her candid tone was blunt, and I loved her directness, unapologetic as the weather." – **Aspen Matis**

"Daughter-in-love can be an honorary title or a hereditary one, either way, come age and arguments, fights and forgiveness, it is a lifetime appointment – **Marie Bostiwick,**

Ecclesiastes: Let us hear the conclusion of the whole matter: Fear God and keep His commandments: for this is the whole duty of man. And we know the new commandment of our Lord and Savior is a follow: Thou shalt love the Lord thy God with all thy heart, and all thy soul, and with all thy strength, with all thy mind, and thy neighbor as thyself. So says the book of Luke chapter ten and verse twenty-seven…including the in-laws!

Allow me to agree with you in prayer concerning your marriage:

Father God in the name of Jesus, I agree with the reader and their spouse of this covenant marriage. I bind the spirit of infirmity, division, and confusion that has been operating in their lives. I declare and decree over their lives and command their spirit to arise and shine for their Light has come. We believe Your Word to be true. We trust Your Spirit and Your Voice. Thank You for making every crooked place straight and bringing down every high mountain. I declare peace in their lives and in their homes. Let love arise in their marriage and every enemy towards their marriage be scattered. I pray for salvation.

and true deliverance throughout both families. Thank You for a healthy marriage as You ordained. We glorify You for change, expansion, deliverance, mercy, and grace in the name of Jesus. We release our most holy faith to bring it to pass as we rest in the finished works of Jesus. In Jesus's name we pray – Amen. – Selah

My dearest readers, I pray something was said that encouraged you to continue to move forward in the Faith! Remember, there is **NOTHING** too hard for God! You are not alone, and Jesus is with you, and He will cause you to triumph in every area of your life. You can dodge every satanic dart thrown at you *AND* your marriage; from your in-laws, or anyone else. Go and maintain what Christ has obtained for you. You have the Victory, and you will experience a supernatural change from parent in-laws; siblings in-laws to parent in-

loves; and sibling in-loves as well. It is so in
Jesus' name – Amen.

ACKNOWLEDGEMENTS

A special dedication to my daddy who went home to be with the Lord in 2019. Thank you for loving me with an everlasting unconditional love. Because of you, I understand and embrace the love of my Heavenly Father. I love you daddy, to infinity and beyond.

I honor & acknowledge my husband Melvin Lewis Amos, Jr. You promised to be my husband at an early age. Like "WOW" the miracle still blows my mind! Forever is a long time. Thank you for your unyielding support. I love you!

To my mom: thanks mom, you raised me to know that in God, I am UNSINKABLE! I love you more than words can express. Thank you for being the epitome of LOVE in action.

To the rest of my Family of Victory:
Adrien, Phyllis, Tisca, Ashley, Amber,
Roman, Ambriel, Adrien, and Ari-Samuel,
Sasha, Tatyanna, Emmanuel, Ralph, Tank,
Amari, Aunt Vera, Uncle Sam.
To my bonus children, Father and mother
in-love, Mr. Melvin & Marlene Amos Sr.,
present and past sibling in laws-in-love – I
love you all to infinity and beyond. A
special God bless you to my spiritual
children throughout the world.
Thank you to my assigned Prophet – Dr.
Franklin Battle Sr. who made sure I knew
my true identity.
To my World Changers family. "As we
understand grace, we empower change."
Pastor Carol Jones, Pastor Mike Jones,
Pastor Edward & Modistine Risper; Mr. Bill
& Mrs. Marilyn Lewis, Mr. Edward & Mrs.
Carolyn Lewis, continued blessings. To our
marriage advisor Deacon Claude Davis,
thank you for listening ears and prayers.
To my special friends:

State Representative Miriam Lucas Paris,
Apostle Jerome, and Lady Morgan Dukes;
thank you and I love and appreciate you
more than you know.
I am eternally blessed and grateful for Dr.
Janet Hogan – Lamar, CEO of Queen
Esther Mega Networks & Marketing Agency
for believing in me and pushing me out of
my comfort zone from behind the scenes.
Apostle Robert E. Knight Jr., Pastor Alvin &
Dr. Patricia Stanley; The Late Overseer
Willie Frazier, The Photographer – continue
to sleep in peace… and the entire Network;
there are no words to express the depth of
love I have within for ALL of you! I am
ETERNALLY GRATEFUL *for each of you.*

About The Author

SHANNON STAFFORD – AMOS

is the daughter of Mr. & Mrs. Wallace and Charlotte Denson. She is an original *Georgia Peach*. She was born at Grady Memorial Hospital and educated through the Dekalb County School system. She attended Georgia State University, MED, Ministerial

Education Development Pastoral Leadership at World Changers Church Int'l. Lady Amos is a graduate of Draughon's College of Nursing and Georgia MLS Estate Institute. Minister Shannon is married to her childhood sweetheart, Melvin Amos Jr. They reside in the Middle Georgia area. Minister Shannon is a devoted mom to Ashley and Amber. She has been blessed with four grandchildren; a bonus mom to four children; and a spiritual mother to dozens in the Body of Christ.

Minister Shannon facilitates The Families of Victory program in Macon, Georgia. She has been blessed to serve the great state of Georgia's residential and commercial consumers as a licensed realtor and with Tuggle House Properties LLC for over 25 years!

As the CEO of Stafford Ministry Services, Minister Shannon is in great demand for speaking engagements; both national and international, as well as a ministry service facilitator, and for family conferences. Minister Shannon has made radio, tv, and podcast guest appearances. She's been a host/co-host as well in those same arenas. She is the creative & founding host of the Families of Victory Broadcast.

SHANNON STAFFORD – AMOS

www.shannonstafford.org

Families of Victory: 678 – 770 – 1952

Stafford Services: 478 – 951 – 4655

Email: shannonstafford7@ymail.com

www.ingramcontent.com/pod-product-compliance
Lightning Source LLC
Chambersburg PA
CBHW060833250626
47162CB00005B/2048